This igloo book belongs to:

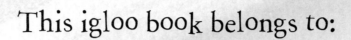

....

igloobooks

Published in 2015
by Igloo Books Ltd
Cottage Farm
Sywell
NN6 0BJ
www.igloobooks.com

SHE001 0715
2 4 6 8 10 9 7 5 3
ISBN: 978-1-78343-304-9

Printed and manufactured in China

My Treasury of
Stories
for
Boys

igloobooks

Contents

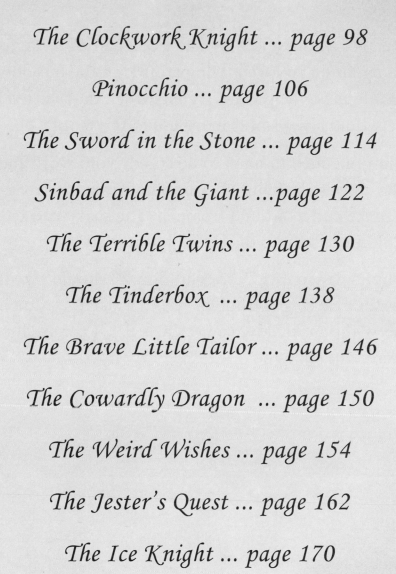

The Knight and the Dragon

Along time ago, a Lord and Lady had a son named John. John hated work of any kind and loved lazing around in the meadows outside the town. He never helped his parents when they visited the local townspeople. He would always find an excuse to stay home.

One Sunday, John pretended to be ill so he could avoid work and spend all day playing in the woods. As John was climbing a tree, he saw a strange-looking snake curled around a branch. The snake had red scales and sharp little teeth. John picked up the snake, but it tried to bite him.

"This snake might be dangerous," thought John. "I should take it home and cage it, so that it can't cause any trouble." But the snake was too slippery to hold, so John threw the snake down a nearby well. "I'm sure it can't hurt anyone down there," he thought.

The Knight and the Dragon

Years passed and the snake in the well grew bigger and bigger.
It grew scales and horns and great feet with claws as big as knives.
And the sharp teeth also got bigger and bigger too. Soon, the snake wasn't
a snake any more, it was a dragon!

One day, the dragon crept out of the well and snapped up insects and birds.
As it grew even larger and larger, it started eating rabbits, then deer, until it
was sneaking into fields and stealing sheep.

One night, it curled its long body around a hill behind the local town and went to sleep. When the townspeople saw the dragon the next morning, they were terrified. They marched to the manor house and banged on the door. "You must save us from the dragon!" they cried.

When the dragon awoke it slithered down to the manor house. Puffs of flame shot from its nostrils and a hiss-like steam came from its gaping jaws. When the townspeople saw, they banged on the manor house's door. A sleepy butler unlocked the great door and was surprised when all the townspeople rushed in, slamming the door behind them. The dragon howled and stamped outside in a rage.

The lady of the manor had a clever idea. She asked the townspeople to run to the dairy and pour all the day's milk into a deep trough. When the dragon saw the milk, it drank it all up and looked around for more. When it saw there wasn't any more, it roared and crept back to its hill to sleep.

Every day from then on, the dragon drank all the town's milk and slept, but it still ripped up meadows, knocked down houses and scared the sheep and cows. Many knights and heroes came to defeat the dragon, but the dragon always won.

Meanwhile, John had become a great knight. When he retuned home and his parents told him about the dragon, he looked out at the dragon's hill. He realised that the dragon was the snake he had found all those years ago.

John's parents told him all about the heroes who had failed to defeat the dragon, but John knew what to do. "This is a special type of monster," he said, "and it will need something special to defeat it." He spoke to the town's blacksmith and asked him to make him a new suit of armor with some very unusual parts.

The next day, the forge in the town rang with the sound of steel, as the blacksmith made the special armor. Nobody had ever seen armor like it before. It had spikes jutting out of it at all angles. When it was complete, John put it on. He looked a fearsome sight.

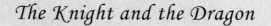

Clanking and creaking, John walked to the dragon's hill. He waved his sword and shouted at the dragon. The dragon raised its ugly head and roared, then slid off the hill.

John marched towards the dragon, shouting all the time. Quick as a flash, the dragon wound its body around John. John swiped his sword at the dragon's head, but it was too fast for him. He couldn't hit it at all.

The dragon began to squeeze and squeeze, but the spikes on John's armor dug into it, hurting it. The harder the dragon squeezed, the more it hurt. Instead of running away, or using its fearsome flames, the foolish dragon just kept on squeezing.

The battle continued all day, until the dragon was so tired and hurt, that it uncoiled itself and slithered away, never to return.

The townspeople were overjoyed. They were safe at last. John became a hero and everyone lived happily ever after.

Dick Whittington and his Cat

Once upon a time, there was a poor boy named Dick Whittington. Dick's parents had died when he was very little, so he was very poor and alone.

One day, as he was begging for food, Dick heard two villagers talking. "The streets of London are paved with gold," said one to the other.

Dick decided to go to London. "If the streets are paved with gold, I will make my fortune there," he thought.

Dick travelled for many days, until he reached London. However, the streets of London weren't paved with gold. Everything was noisy, dirty and smelly and there was no work anywhere.

Dick was very tired and hungry. He rested on the doorstep of a grand house. He woke to find a grumpy cook staring at him. "Be off with you!" she cried. "We'll have no tramps here."

"Wait," said a kindly voice. It was the master of the house. "What's the matter, boy?"

Dick told the master that he was looking for work and had no food.

The man, whose name was Mr Fitzwarren, gave Dick a job, working in his kitchen. Dick was very happy and decided to work as hard as he could. Mr Fitzwarren's daughter, Alice, took pity on him, and gave him scraps of fine food from her meals.

However, life was still very hard for Dick. The cook treated him badly and made him do all the hardest work. His little room in the loft of the house was filled with rats and mice, which scampered over his bed at night, so he could never get to sleep.

Early one morning, in an alley outside the house, Dick saw a cold, thin and hungry-looking kitten. Taking pity on it, he gave her some of his food. The kitten purred and jumped into his arms. From that moment, the kitten followed Dick everywhere. She grew up to be a sleek and elegant cat. Every night, the cat would come up to Dick's room and chase away all the rats and mice.

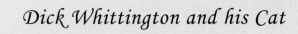

Mr Fitzwarren was a rich merchant who sent ships across the sea to far-off lands. The ships were full of things to sell and when they returned, they were always full of gold. Everyone in Mr Fitzwarren's house was allowed to put something on the ship to sell far away, to see if it would bring them money. Only Dick had nothing to put on the ship.

"Why not put your cat on board?" said Alice to Dick. "Someone may want to buy her."

Dick was sad to see his cat go, but he put her on board Mr Fitzwarren's ship before it sailed away.

From that day on, Dick was lonelier than ever. The cook treated him even worse than before and now there was no cat to keep away the rats and mice.

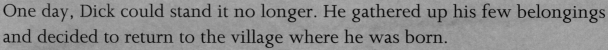

One day, Dick could stand it no longer. He gathered up his few belongings and decided to return to the village where he was born.

"London is too hard a place for me," he thought, sadly, as he crossed the hills that led away from the city. Just then, the bells of the great church at Bow began to peal. Dick stopped. "Turn again, Whittington, Lord Mayor of London," they seemed to be saying.

"Could I really be Lord Mayor, one day?" said Dick, turning back towards the city. "Then I will stay in London." He ran back down the hill and was back at Mr Fitzwarren's house, before anyone even knew he had left.

Meanwhile, Dick's little cat was travelling across the sea in the big ship. The ship was filled with rats and mice that nibbled at all the food in the ship's kitchen. The cat guarded the food, so the rats and mice could not get it.

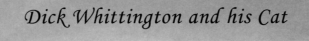

The crew fed her well in thanks. "That cat is the best mouser we've ever seen," they said.

Months passed and the ship crossed the waves and reached a far-off land. A great and powerful queen lived there, but her palace was overrun with rats.

When the crew sat to eat with the queen, hundreds of rats dashed out of holes, scampered onto the table, and ate all the food. "I wish there was something that would stop these creatures," said the queen.

One of the crew remembered Dick's cat, who was asleep on board the ship. He fetched the cat and brought it to the queen.

As soon as the cat saw the rats, it leapt onto the table and chased them all away. The rats were so terrified that they hurried out of the palace and never came back.

The queen was delighted. "I will give the owner of this cat a thousand pieces of gold!" she said. She then gave the cat a collar made of solid gold and returned it to the ship. When the ship sailed back to London, Mr Fitzwarren took the chest of gold to Dick, who was scrubbing the floors in the kitchen.

"Dick," said Mr Fitzwarren, "your cat has come back and she's earned you more money than I have ever seen!" Dick couldn't believe his eyes. With the chest of gold, he was suddenly the richest man in London. He generously gave gold pieces to all the people who had helped him while he was poor. He even gave some to the cook, who stopped being quite so grumpy.

Now Dick was rich, he bought the finest house in London and eventually married Alice who had been so kind to him while he was poor. The words of Bow Bells came true as well. Dick Whittington became a prosperous merchant and when he was older, he became Lord Mayor of London. However, he never forgot that it was all thanks to his little cat.

Sir Gawaine and the Green Knight

It was Christmas in the castle of Camelot. King Arthur and his knights were celebrating with a great feast. Fires flickered and the tables groaned under the weight of the food. All the knights and their ladies were laughing and joking.

Suddenly, the door of the Great Hall flew open and a giant knight rode in. He was covered in green armor. His eyes seemed to glow like emeralds. His beard was like a tangle of twigs and leaves. Even his horses coat was a deep, mossy green. He carried a sharp axe made of some strange green metal. It was almost as big as he was. Bright holly berries grew around the handle.

King Arthur and his knights sat in silence as the strange knight said, "I challenge one of you to a battle to the death. You must strike me first. Then you must promise that I will have a chance to strike you back. Are any of you beardless little boys brave enough to fight me?"

"Sir Gawaine was the most courageous of Arthur's knights. He rose to his feet. "I accept." he said. So, the green knight got off his horse.

Sir Gawaine swung his sword and chopped at the the green knight's head.

He did not know that the strange knight was enchanted and instead of falling over, the green knight calmly picked up his head.

"In a year and a day," said the head, "you must promise to find me in the green chapel. It will only appear to you if you do not hunt, or kill. Then it will be my turn to strike you." The green knight got on his horse and thundered out of the castle, carrying his head.

"I must find the green chapel," Sir Gawaine said, "And let the green knight strike me with his axe."

"But he'll kill you," said King Arthur.

"A promise is a promise," said Sir Gawaine, sadly. "A knight always keeps his word."

Nobody in Camelot had ever heard of the green chapel. So Sir Gawaine rode across England all through spring and summer, trying to find it.

As the leaves started to fall from the trees, Sir Gawaine rode into an old, dark forest. In those days, there were still many wild and terrible creatures roaming the forest. Sir Gawaine had to fight off twisting green dragons that nested in the roots of trees. He scared wolves away with fire. He even had to fend off the wild men of the woods, who were half-tree, half-man. But he did not hunt, or kill any wild animal, because he knew that if he did, he would never enter the green chapel.

After many adventures, Sir Gawaine came to a great mansion in the middle of the forest. A friendly, red-cheeked man opened the door to him. Sir Gawaine asked if he had heard of the green chapel.

"I am Sir Bertilak," the man said. "The green chapel is a short distance away. Stay with us until the year is done. All I ask is that you come hunting with me."

Sir Bertilak's wife was a beautiful lady. "Fetch me a deer, Sir Gawaine and prove you are the best knight in the land," she said.

So, the next day, Sir Gawaine went hunting with Sir Bertilak. Sir Gawaine saw a beautiful deer. But Sir Gawaine knew he could not kill it, or he would never enter the green chapel. He pretended to get his arrows ready and the deer ran off.

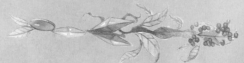

"Fetch me a boar," said Sir Bertilak's wife on the second day.

Sir Gawaine found a huge wild boar, deep in the forest. It charged with its deadly tusks, but Sir Gawaine batted it away with his sword and it disappeared back into the forest.

"There is a red fox in the wood," Sir Bertilak's wife said on the third day. "Anyone who wears its skin will be safe from axe blows."

Sir Bertilak and Sir Gawaine went into the forest and found the fox drinking at a pool. This time, Sir Gawaine aimed his bow and, by mistake, he shot an arrow at the fox, but it swiftly ran away.

The next day, it was a year and a day since Sir Gawaine's promise. He rode to the green chapel and found a high sheet of rock, covered in ivy. Sir Gawaine placed his hand on the rock and it parted, letting him inside.

Sir Gawaine and the Green Knight

The green chapel was a cavern, deep in the earth. Its walls sparkled with emeralds and deep tree roots. The green knight was waiting for him. His head was back on his shoulders.

"Lay your head down on this stone," boomed the green knight, "and I'll strike my blow."

Trembling, Sir Gawaine knelt down and put his head on the cold stone. The green knight brought down the axe—right to the edge of Gawaine's neck. "A bad stroke," said the green knight. "Let me try again." He brought the axe down a second time and stopped it once more on Gawaine's neck. "One last time," said the green knight. "And this time, I will strike."

The green knight brought the axe down for a third time. It just grazed Sir Gawaine's neck, leaving a tiny mark.

"Now you have struck me and the bargain is complete!" shouted Sir Gawaine. "Let's fight like men." He drew his sword. But the green knight was laughing.

"I am Sir Bertilak," said the green knight. "Or rather, he is me. I am the guardian of the enchanted forest. I decided to test your trustworthiness by seeing whether you would hunt my precious wild animals. The first and second times, you did not. On the third time, you shot an arrow at my fox. That is why my third strike touched your neck. But you have proved your goodness. You didn't break your promise, even though you thought it meant certain death. Arthur's knights are truly the greatest in the land."

Sir Gawaine rode home, amazed to have survived. When he told King Arthur and his knights about his adventure, they all decided to wear green ribbons, so that none of them would forget Sir Gawaine's courage, or the story of the green knight.

The Sea Serpent

Once upon a time, a gigantic sea serpent lived near many islands. The serpent was as big as ten dragons. Its eyes were the size of lakes and each of its teeth was as high as a tower. When it raised its head above the water, it made huge waves crash into the cliffs of the nearby islands. And when it roared, everyone could hear it for miles around.

One day, the king of one of the islands looked out and saw that the waves crashing by his cliffside castle were much higher than usual. He watched as the great sea serpent raised its head out of the water, until its eyes were as high as the king's tower. The king leaned out of his castle window and shook his fist at the sea serpent. "Be gone, foul beast!" he cried. But the serpent let out a roar that almost shook the castle apart.

The king sent out his chief wizard to see if he could enchant the sea serpent away, but the old wizard was powerless. The serpent roared at the wizard, who ran back to the castle before the sea serpent could eat him up.

This wizard was a very wise and clever man who could understand the speech of sea serpents. When he spoke to the king, he trembled almost as much as he had done when he had seen the sea serpent. "Sire," said the wizard. "The sea serpent is angry at your insult to it. It says he will only go away if he is given your only daughter to eat. If he does not have her, he will destroy your castle."

The king was scared, as well as angry now. However, he made his heralds ride all over the island with a proclamation; "Anyone who can kill the sea serpent can have my sword, my daughter's hand in marriage and my kingdom when I die."

Soon, many brave knights came to the island to try and slay the sea serpent. Some had killed dragons before, but the sea serpent was much, much bigger. When most of them saw the sea serpent, they ran away.

The Sea Serpent

The bravest ones tried to defeat it, but they only knew how to fight on land. Their armor was too heavy and they were soon gobbled up by the monstrous serpent.

At this time, a farmer and his wife lived on the island with their seven sons. The sons were all lively, active young men, apart from the youngest. He was small and thin and liked to dream about adventures as he sat at the fireside. His older brothers loved to tease and bully him.

When the family heard about the sea serpent, the youngest brother said "I can defeat it," very quietly. Everyone laughed at him. "You can't even hold a shield, or swing a sword!" said his brothers.

"I don't need a sword, or shield, to defeat the sea serpent," said the youngest brother, staring into the fire. The family didn't listen. They thought that the boy had got caught up in one of his own stories.

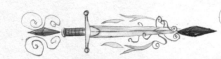

But the youngest brother was cleverer than he looked. When everyone had gone to bed and the fire had died down, he picked up a square of peat from the fire. Peat burns very slowly and the boy saw that there was still a tiny spark of flame in the middle of it.

The youngest brother took the peat and went out to the stable, where his father's horse stood. He got on the horse and galloped as fast as he could to the castle where the sea serpent waited. It was almost dawn when he reached a port near the castle. He found a small rowing boat and got in it, carrying only the peat.

Then, the youngest brother rowed as fast as he could out to the sea serpent, which was laying with its gigantic mouth half in the water. The sea serpent was sleeping and every so often it opened its mouth and yawned.

The youngest brother waited until the sea serpent yawned again and then rowed the boat right inside the sea serpent's mouth. Suddenly, the boat was floating down the sea serpent's throat at top speed, splashing and rocking. The boy held on tight until the boat came to rest in the sea serpent's belly.

It was very dark and smelly in the beast's stomach. The only light was the tiny flame from the lump of peat. The youngest brother blew gently on the flame and it slowly grew, until the belly was lit up with the fire. It was like a great, red cavern. Then he put the burning peat down next to a pile of wood from a ship that the sea serpent had swallowed. It soon caught flame and burned merrily.

The sea serpent felt the fire in its belly and woke up. Its stomach started to twist and shudder like an earthquake. The boy got back in the boat and rowed back towards the beast's mouth. As the serpent roared with pain, he rowed right out of its mouth again.

The sea serpent was burning up from inside. It snaked its head at the boat and tried to crush the boy in its jaws. Luckily, he managed to avoid its attacks and rowed as fast as he could towards the shore. With one last mighty roar, the sea serpent died and its head smashed back into the water.

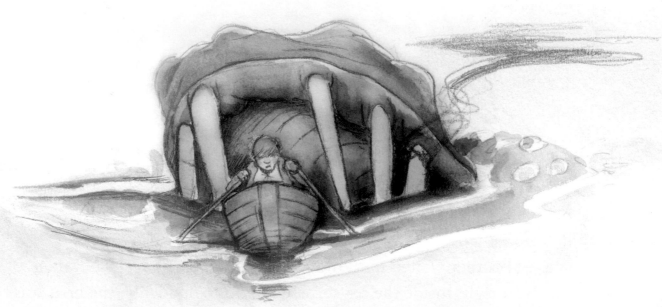

The wave carried the youngest brother all the way back to the port. When the people on the land saw what the youngest brother had done, they took him to the king and he was proclaimed a great hero.

The youngest brother married the king's daughter and took the king's sword. But he didn't forget his family. He invited them all to come and live in the castle with him and he made sure his throne was near a great fire, just like his place near the hearth at his old home. So the youngest brother, the princess and all their family lived happily ever after.

The Knight's Tower

Once there was a kind young man called Thomas, the youngest of three brothers. His two older brothers had both gone into the world to seek their fortunes. They were known far and wide as brave young men who fought monsters and rescued maidens.

Thomas longed to be a hero, just like his brothers, but he didn't know how. "If only I could find out what the secret of being a hero is," he thought, sadly.

One day, Thomas was walking along a forest path when he saw a strange old man who had fallen down in a puddle. Thomas helped him up. "In return for your kindness," said the old man, "I will answer any question you ask."

"How do I become a hero?" asked Thomas.
The old man smiled crookedly. "There is only one person who can tell you that," he said. "You must ask the knight who lives at the top of the tall tower, in the depths of the woods."

Thomas was puzzled by the old man's words, but he thanked him anyway and then set off into the woods. He hadn't gone far before he heard a strange, whining sound. Thomas followed the sound, which seemed to be coming from a clearing near the trees.

The Knight's Tower

Thomas reached the clearing, and found a wolf that was whining. Thomas was about to run away, when he saw that the wolf had a thorn in its paw.

"If I help it, it may try to bite me," thought Thomas, but he plucked the thorn from the wolf's paw anyway.

"Thank you, stranger," said the wolf, in a soft voice. "Can I help you?"

"I'm looking for the knight's tower," said Thomas.

"I will show you the way," said the wolf. Thomas followed the wolf deep into the forest. "This is as far as I will go," the wolf said and disappeared back into the woods.

Thomas carried on walking, until he heard another sound. It was a great groaning and growling. Pushing through the trees, Thomas found a great brown bear that had caught its paw under a fallen tree. "If I help it, it may chase me when it's free," thought Thomas. But he helped the bear to pull it's paw out anyway.

Instead of attacking Thomas, the bear asked, "What can I do for you?" Thomas told him about the knight's tower. "I will carry you to the tower," said the bear. "Climb on my back."

Thomas climbed on the bear's back. It ran through the forest until it reached a tower that was so high above the trees, its top was lost in the clouds.

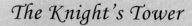

The bear ran back into the forest while Thomas looked all around the tower. He saw that it had no door, or windows. It was impossible to get inside.

Thomas heard a low, rumbling roar. Following the sound, Thomas found a great, green dragon. It had been caught in a landslide and one of its wings was trapped under a big pile of rocks. "If I help the dragon, it will surely eat me," thought Thomas. But the dragon seemed so sad and hurt, that Thomas couldn't leave it. He took rocks off the dragon's wing, until it was free again.

The dragon reared up and flapped its wings and Thomas was afraid that it would heat him up. But the dragon asked, "How may I thank you?" Thomas explained about the knight's tower.

"Climb on my back," said the dragon. Thomas was scared, but he did as the dragon suggested. Thomas clung on to the dragon's neck and it flew up into the clouds. Above the clouds, Thomas saw a small ledge and a door at the top of the tower. The dragon flew to the ledge and Thomas stepped onto it.

The door was opened by a knight in gleaming armor. He invited Thomas into the tower. "Great knight," asked Thomas, "how can I become a hero?"

"A hero has kindness," said the knight. "Did you help the wolf in the woods?"
"Yes," said Thomas.
"A hero has spirit," said the knight. "Did you ride the bear?"
"Yes," said Thomas.
"And, most of all, a hero has courage," said the knight, "did you fly up here with the dragon?"

"I did," said Thomas.

"Then you are a hero already," the knight said. "At the bottom of the tower, you will find gifts fit for a hero."

The dragon flew Thomas back down to the bottom of the tower. A proud, black horse and a shining suit of armor were waiting for him.

Thomas put the suit of armor on and rode the black horse through the forest to seek his fortune. After many adventures, Thomas made his fortune and became the greatest hero in the land and lived happily ever after.

The Pirate Prince

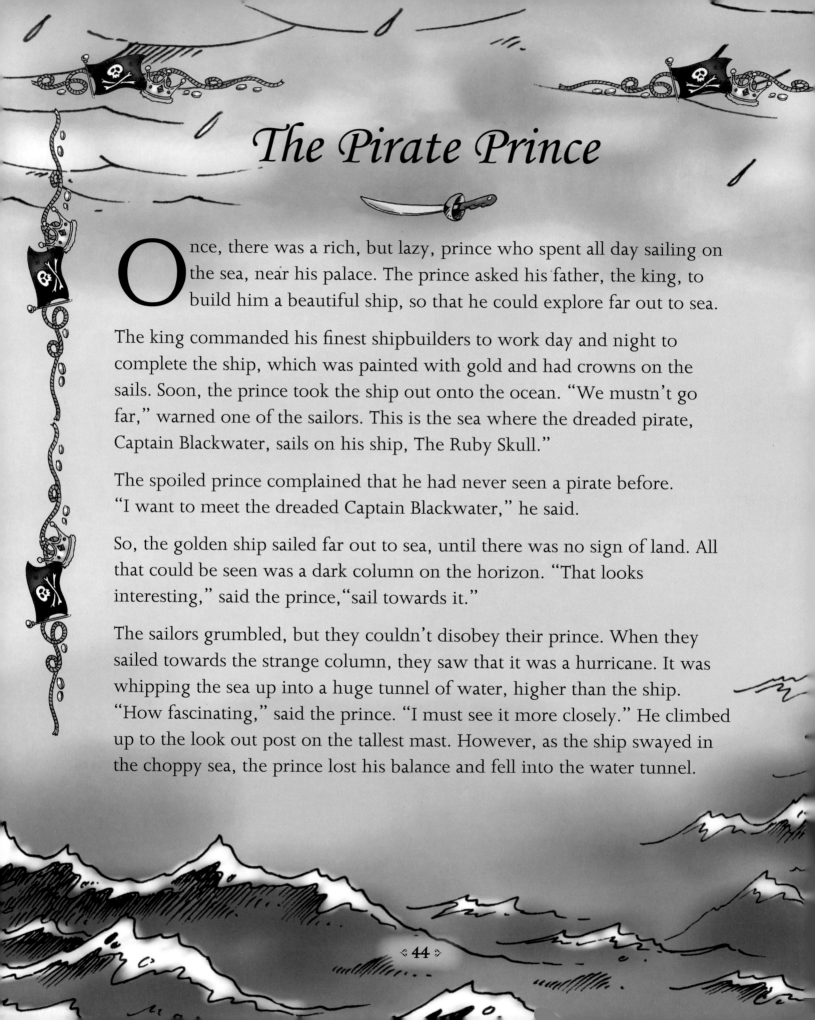

Once, there was a rich, but lazy, prince who spent all day sailing on the sea, near his palace. The prince asked his father, the king, to build him a beautiful ship, so that he could explore far out to sea.

The king commanded his finest shipbuilders to work day and night to complete the ship, which was painted with gold and had crowns on the sails. Soon, the prince took the ship out onto the ocean. "We mustn't go far," warned one of the sailors. This is the sea where the dreaded pirate, Captain Blackwater, sails on his ship, The Ruby Skull."

The spoiled prince complained that he had never seen a pirate before. "I want to meet the dreaded Captain Blackwater," he said.

So, the golden ship sailed far out to sea, until there was no sign of land. All that could be seen was a dark column on the horizon. "That looks interesting," said the prince, "sail towards it."

The sailors grumbled, but they couldn't disobey their prince. When they sailed towards the strange column, they saw that it was a hurricane. It was whipping the sea up into a huge tunnel of water, higher than the ship. "How fascinating," said the prince. "I must see it more closely." He climbed up to the look out post on the tallest mast. However, as the ship swayed in the choppy sea, the prince lost his balance and fell into the water tunnel.

The prince was sucked into the hurricane and carried far away until, at last, the fierce wind died down and the prince was dropped into the sea. He swam with all his might and eventually reached a deserted island.

The prince lived on the empty island for many months, growing lean and fit. One day, a big, fast-looking ship sailed past. The prince waved and shouted at the top of his voice. The ship stopped and he swam out to it.

A rope dropped down the side of the great ship and the prince climbed up. Someone helped him, but instead of grabbing onto a hand, the prince found he was holding a hook. It belonged to none other than Captain Blackwater, the most fearsome pirate on the seven seas. The ship was his famous vessel, The Ruby Skull.

"We have come to this island to maroon a group of mutineers," said the captain. "One of them was my second in command. If you can defeat him in a swordfight, you can take his place."

The mutinous sailor was a wicked-looking man. Someone threw the prince a sword and he fought the sailor on the deck of The Ruby Skull. With a clever flick of his sword, the prince sent the man tumbling over the side of the ship and the pirates gave a big cheer.

"There is a wicked sultan in these parts who kidnaps men from the coast and sells them as slaves," said Captain Blackwater. "We plunder his ships and set the slaves free. Will you join us, stranger?"

The prince had no choice but to join Captain Blackwater's crew and became a pirate. They sailed the seas and attacked all the sultan's ships they could find. They stole all the gold and jewels from the sultan and they set all the sultan's slaves free. The prince became a hardworking sailor and a brave fighter. He soon lost his spoiled ways.

One day, news reached Captain Blackwater that the sultan had sent boats out to capture a king, who was sailing nearby.

"This king sails the ocean in a golden ship, with crowns on the sails," said the captain. "It's said that he searches for his long-lost son."

When the prince heard this, he knew this king must be his father. "I know this king," said the prince. "If we can reach him before the sultan does, we will all be rich."

"The sultan's ship is twice as big as The Ruby Skull," said Captain Blackwater. "We must reach the king's ship first."

The captain set sail for the golden ship but, as it came within sight, the prince saw that the sultan's towering vessel had already reached it.

The sultan's men had jumped aboard the king's ship and taken him hostage.

Captain Blackwater waited until the dead of night, then he sailed up close and sneaked aboard with all his crew.

When the sultan's men woke up, they found they were being invaded. They drew their weapons and fought the pirates. In the chaos of the battle, the prince searched the lower deck of the ship until he found a locked room. Forcing it open, he found the king inside. The king drew his sword. "You won't take me alive, pirate," he roared.

"I'm here to rescue you, father," said the prince. The king recognized his son and they hugged, joyfully. Together, the king and the prince rushed to fight with Captain Blackwater and his men. They helped the pirates to defeat the sultan's crew and capture the huge ship.

When the battle was over, Captain Blackwater was very surprised to find that a member of his crew was a prince. However, he was a little worried that the king might punish him for his pirate ways.

The next day, the king, the prince and the pirates all sailed back to the palace together. The king was so delighted to have his son back, he made Captain Blackwater head of his fleet. The captain was so proud, he decided to give up being a pirate altogether.

After that, the sultan never troubled the king, or the pirate prince again and everyone lived happily ever after.

The Grimwort Ghosts

The Grimworts were different from other families. They liked dark dungeons and slimy cellars, where no light ever reached. They liked cobwebs and spiders and things that go bump in the night, because the Grimworts weren't ordinary people, they were ghosts.

In an ancient tower, in the middle of a very old city, the Grimworts happily haunted the draughty stairwells and creepy corridors. They loved nothing more than to scare the socks off any visitors who came to call. They especially liked frightening children, because they seemed to scream longer and louder than adults. In fact, the louder the children screamed, the funnier the Grimworts found it. All day long, they lurked silently in the shadows, waiting for their next victim to pass by.

However, the mischievous ghost family had a problem. Egor, the youngest ghost wasn't very good at frightening people. He just couldn't get the hang of it.

His parents were very worried. "Do a blood-curdling scream," said Lord Grimwort, one day. So, Egor opened his mouth, as wide as he could, but for some reason, the tiniest, squeakiest, "Oooooooh," sound came out.

Lord and Lady Grimwort looked at each other in a very worried fashion. "Really, Egor," said his mother, "what is the point of being a ghost if you can't scare people?"

Lord Grimwort stood up. A really good, blood-curdling scream sounds like this," he said, opening his mouth so wide, you could see what he'd eaten for breakfast three hundred years ago, when he was still alive.

"AAAARGH!" he screamed. The rats in the dungeon ran for cover and the bats dropped from the ceiling. Egor put his fingers in his ears. His father's screams were really deafening.

The Grimwort Ghosts

< 53 >

The Grimwort Ghosts

"I can rattle my chains," said Egor, "they're scary." He gave his chains a good shake, but they just sounded like a baby shaking its rattle.

"Oh, dear," said Lady Grimwort, disappearing through the dungeon wall. "Whatever are we to do with you, Egor?"

Lord Grimwort looked at the clock. "Some children are coming to see the dungeons this afternoon. Let's give them the fright of their lives," he said, with a dastardly cackle.

Everyone got ready for the haunting. Egor's brother, Oswald, slipped into his costume with bloodstains down the front. "I like scaring children," he cackled. Edmund put on a black hood with slits for eyes. He picked up his executioner's axe, swung it high in the air and waved it around.

"Come on," said Lord Grimwort, "it's time to get to our places."

Lady Grimwort put on her 'lady about to be beheaded' costume, practised one of her spine-chilling wails and the whole family moved off in the direction of the dungeons.

The dungeons were dark and dank, and eerie shadows slunk in corners. Lord Grimwort suddenly pointed at a rotting, old, empty barrel. "This is what I want you do, Egor," he said. "I want you to hide in this big wooden barrel and when the children come in, I want you to pop your head up and give them a nasty fright."

Egor's father lifted him into the barrel. "Where will you be?" Egor asked. "We're going to terrify the tour guides further down the passage," said Lord Grimwort with a happy smile. Lady Grimwort kissed Egor. "Be my spookiest son, darling," she said.

The Grimwort Ghosts

Egor settled down and waited. It was comfy in the barrel, but a little too warm for Egor. He liked things nice and chilly. After a few minutes, Egor's eyes started to close. He was almost asleep when he heard noises. "Ugh, this is horrid," said a girl's voice.

"It's creepy," said another voice. "Imagine being imprisoned down here."

"What are those rings on the wall for?" asked a boy with glasses.

"Prisoners were chained there, long ago, and then left to rot," said the teacher. The children looked around. The dungeon was sinister and they didn't like the way it made shivers run down their spines.

Inside the barrel, Egor stood up behind the classmates. He blew his cold, ghostly breath over them. The children felt the hairs standing up on their arms and the backs of their necks, but they didn't know why.

Egor slunk down into the barrel and then jumped up, suddenly. "Whoo!" he wailed and ducked down again. Everyone turned to look.

"Was that you, Adrian?" asked the teacher, looking at a boy with spiky hair.

"No, Miss Jones," said Adrian, glancing nervously around.

Egor rose up again. "Whoo!" he moaned, right in front of the children. Their mouths fell open and their eyes nearly popped out of their heads. Adrian's spiky hair stood up so high, he looked like a hedgehog. The children all screamed at once.

Egor was so surprised, he fell back inside the barrel and banged his chin. "Oooh," he cried, with a long, mournful moan, "Ooooooh!" The sound echoed in the barrel and seemed to move all around the dark, dank dungeon.

The children were rigid with fright. Then suddenly, they started screaming again and made a mad dash for the door. "Wait," called the teacher, nervously, beginning to run after them. They didn't stop running until they were outside in the warm sunshine.

Egor's family listened with glee from further down the passage.
"What terrifying screams," said Lord Grimwort, "how marvellous."

Lady Grimwort put a big bandage on Egor's sore chin and got his favourite tin whistle for him to play. "I think I'm getting the hang of being a proper ghost," he said. "I'm looking forward to haunting tonight."

After that, visitors to the old tower were more scared than ever. They said that they felt cold breaths of air that sent shivers down their spines and heard eerie noises coming from the dungeons. Little did they know that, at last, Egor really had become a Grimwort ghost.

The Sorcerer's Apprentice

Once there was a young boy who was apprenticed to a powerful sorcerer. The apprentice wanted to learn all the magic that he could so that, one day, he too would be as powerful as the sorcerer himself. The apprentice worked hard for the sorcerer for one year, but during all that time, the sorcerer didn't teach the apprentice a single spell. The apprentice spent his days washing the floors of the sorcerer's drafty castle and cleaning the glass containers that the sorcerer used to mix potions in. Sometimes, the leftover potions would mix together with a 'pop', or make an especially bad smell, or even form a laughing face from smoke that soon drifted apart. But this was the nearest the apprentice ever came to magic.

"Master, when will I learn to do magic like you?" the apprentice asked, one day "Maybe I could conjure up a little fireball. Or learn to fly, maybe? Just a little way off the ground?"

"Magic is about hard work and study, not flights and explosions," the sorcerer replied, locking his spellbook safely in his cabinet. "You're here to learn real magic, not stage tricks. Now, get back to work." The sorcerer was a very grave and stern man and the apprentice was a little afraid of him. So the apprentice carried on with his cleaning, but he still longed to cast some real spells.

One day, the sorcerer told the apprentice that he would have to go away for a few days and while he was gone, he wanted the Great Hall cleaned.

The apprentice looked around the Great Hall in dismay. The floor was encrusted with grime. There were dirty cauldrons and dusty glass beakers piled up everywhere. Even the stuffed animal heads on the wall were covered in cobwebs. It was going to take a long time to clean.

The sorcerer departed and the apprentice found a mop and filled a pail of water from the well outside. He began to scrub one corner of the floor, rubbing all the dirt off and making it shine. After an hour or two, he stood up and stretched his aching back. He had only cleaned a tiny part of the floor. The rest was as dirty as ever.

The apprentice left his mop and wandered around the workshop. He was surprised to see that his master's cabinet was unlocked. Peering inside, he saw the sorcerer's spellbook. He was not allowed to touch the spellbook, or even look inside it because it was the source of all the sorcerer's power.

"A small look can't hurt," thought the apprentice. He took the spellbook from the cabinet and opened it. It fell open on a page with a spell that made household objects move around. "Hmm," thought the apprentice. "I wonder if the mop could do the sweeping for me."

The apprentice recited the words on the page loudly, pointing at the mop. At first, nothing happened. Then the mop shook and picked itself up from the floor. It began scrubbing the floor all by itself. It even slid back to the pail of water and dipped itself in, before returning to its task.

"Fantastic!" cried the apprentice out loud. He pulled up a chair and watched as the mop scrubbed away at the floor. Soon, all the water was gone from the pail, but the mop kept scrubbing away.

The apprentice thumbed through the spellbook and found a spell that made water appear. He cast it on the bucket and instantly it was full to the brim with water and suds.

It wasn't long before the mop had cleaned the whole floor to a sparkling shine. But the mop didn't stop. It went back to the first corner and started cleaning again. The apprentice looked in the spellbook, but there were no instructions on stopping the spell. The mop began to clean faster and faster. It started to swipe at the objects on the long tables, knocking over all kinds of magical equipment.

"Hey! Stop that!" cried the apprentice. He chased the mop around the hall, until he finally grabbed it with both hands. He snapped the mop in two. "That's the end of that," he said.

However it wasn't! The two halves of the mop began to grow and sprout, until there were two full-sized mops instead of one. Both mops rushed around the hall, swiping and smashing.

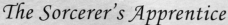

Then the apprentice noticed that his feet were wet. The spell on the bucket was making water pour out of it. It was filling up the room. The apprentice grabbed a hammer and chased the two mops, smashing them to bits. But all the splinters of the mops grew and grew until there were a hundred mops flying through the air.

The water grew so high, the apprentice had to swim. He tried to fight off the mops, but they were everywhere, slashing and swiping and destroying everything in the hall. "If only my master were here!" cried the apprentice in fright.

Suddenly, there was a crack of thunder and a blast of light as the sorcerer appeared. With a wave of his arms, he made the water disappear and with a click of his fingers, the mops fell to the floor and turned back into a single, lifeless mop.

"Please don't turn me into a toad," begged the apprentice, who was still soaking wet.

"I left the cabinet open to see if you could be trusted," the sorcerer said. "I knew you would be meddling with magic as soon as you opened my spellbook, but I didn't return until you had seen what wild magic can do."

"I'm so sorry, Master," said the apprentice. "I'll never dabble in magic without your permission again." The sorcerer made the apprentice clean up the mess with his own hands, but that was all the punishment the apprentice got.

After many years' of hard work, the apprentice became a mighty sorcerer. But he never forgot the lesson that his master had taught him that day.

The Sorcerer's Apprentice

Sir Richard and the Red Knight

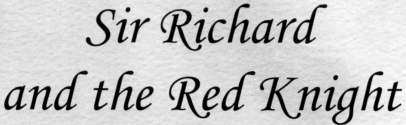

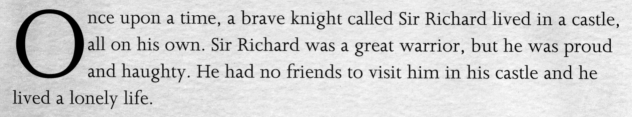

Once upon a time, a brave knight called Sir Richard lived in a castle, all on his own. Sir Richard was a great warrior, but he was proud and haughty. He had no friends to visit him in his castle and he lived a lonely life.

One day, there was a great thump on the castle gate. "Let me in!" a deep voice cried. "I am the Red Knight!"

Sir Richard opened the gate and saw a tremendous sight. It was a man dressed in red armor. Sir Richard was tall, but this man was even taller. He towered over Sir Richard. The Red Knight had a long red beard and red hair and even his eyes seemed to flame and glow.

"Make way, Sir Richard," said the Red Knight, stepping into the empty courtyard of the castle. "I like the look of your castle. I claim it as my own."

"Never!" cried Sir Richard, drawing his long sword. "I challenge you to a duel. If you win, you may take my castle. If you lose, you must leave, never to return."

"Agreed," said the Red Knight and he drew his great, red sword, which glinted dangerously. Sir Richard also drew his sword and the two knights began to fight.

Sir Richard had never fought anyone like the Red Knight before. All his sword blows bounced off the knight's red armor. Even though the Red Knight was so big, he was also very fast. Sir Richard fought bravely, but the Red Knight struck the sword from Sir Richard's hands and threw him to the ground.

Sir Richard had no choice, but to leave his beloved castle with nothing more than the clothes on his back and his sword. He staggered into the woods below the castle, weary and sad.

Day after day, Sir Richard wandered through the woods. He slept under the trees, with a rock for a pillow. Soon, his clothes became tattered and worn and his face grew pinched and pale.

One day, when he had gathered up a small pile of nuts and berries to eat, he heard someone approach. It was a dirty-looking old beggar. "Please," said the beggar, "can you spare some of your food?"

Sir Richard took pity on the poor man and shared his tiny meal. "Thank you," said the beggar. "Let's travel the land together."
Sir Richard agreed and soon he found it was much easier to find food in the forest when there were two people to look.

Some time later, Sir Richard and the beggar found a horse in a clearing. It was the noblest horse the knight had ever seen. Its coat was a silky white and its head was held high. But it was limping from a wound to its front leg.

Sir Richard spoke softly to the horse and bound its leg with a scrap torn from his clothes. "You can join us," he said to the horse and we will take care of you." Sir Richard thought of all the horses he had kept in his stables in the castle and wished he had taken better care of them. "I know what it's like to be cold and hungry now," Sir Richard thought.

As the days passed by, the horse's leg began to get better and before long, it was cantering around happily and nibbling the grass.

One day, as Sir Richard, the beggar and the horse made their way through the woods, they heard a desperate roar. Sir Richard followed the sound and found a great brown bear. One of its paws was caught in a cruel trap. The bear turned its head to Sir Richard and he saw so much pain in its eyes, that he felt he had to help.

Carefully, Sir Richard walked up to the bear. It did not attack him, but only groaned louder. Sir Richard prised open the jaws of the trap with all his might. The bear pulled its paw out of the trap. With a grateful look, it lumbered off into the deep forest.

"That cruel trap must have been set by the Red Knight," said Sir Richard to the beggar. "I wish I could defeat him and win my castle back."

"Perhaps you can," said the beggar. "I was once a great magician before the Red Knight cheated me out of all my riches. I still have some magic left."

The beggar took Sir Richard's old sword and spoke some strange words over it. The sword glowed with an eerie power.
"Now the sword will pierce the Red Knight's armor," said the beggar.

So Sir Richard made the long journey back to his castle, riding on the white horse. He banged on the gate, just as the Red Knight had done.

"Red Knight!" called Sir Richard. "I challenge you. Come out and fight." The Red Knight opened the gate. Sir Richard galloped into the courtyard and the battle began.

The Red Knight was quick, but Sir Richard was on horseback this time and the horse was quicker than the Red Knight. Sir Richard was able to deal the Red Knight some powerful blows with his enchanted sword.

Just when it looked like Sir Richard would beat him, the Red Knight raised his arms and chanted a spell. Sir Richard found himself pulled off the horse. "Now I will kill you!" cried the Red Knight, raising his sword to chop off Sir Richard's head.

Before he could bring the sword down, the Red Knight was knocked over by something huge and brown. It was the bear that Sir Richard had saved from the trap. Together, Sir Richard and the bear drove the Red Knight out of the castle. The Red Knight ran down the hill and far away, defeated at last.

In a flash, the bear turned into a noble knight. "I was cursed by the Red Knight," he said, "but now we have broken his power forever."

So Sir Richard reclaimed his castle at last. He invited the knight and the beggar magician to live with him and the white horse was given a warm stable and all the hay it could eat. With his new friends around him, Sir Richard was never lonely again.

Puss in Boots

Once, there was a miller who had three sons. When it was time for them to go into the world and seek their fortunes, he gave the first son his mill, the second son his donkey, but he had nothing left for his youngest son. "All I have is my cat, Puss," said the boys' father.

So, the youngest son set out into the world, with only the cat for company. "I'll surely starve," he said, sadly.

"No you won't," said the cat. "I will make you a prince, master, if only you'll get me a pair of boots."

The miller's astonished son used the last of his money to buy the cat a pair of shiny, leather boots. Then the cat went into the woods and caught a fine rabbit. Instead of taking it to the miller's son, he travelled all the way to the palace and presented it to the king himself. "It is a present from my lord," said Puss.

The king was impressed. "Who is your lord, little cat?" he asked.
The cat made up a grand-sounding title. "He is the Marquis of Carabas," said Puss.

Month after month, Puss caught the best rabbits he could find and took them to the king, who grew more and more pleased with this mysterious Lord and his cat messenger.

Meanwhile, the miller's son had hardly any food. "When do we eat?" he said. "I've had nothing but crusts for weeks."

"Just go down to the river for a wash," said the cunning cat, "and you'll be surprised."

So, the miller's son went to the river by the big bridge, to wash himself. The cat knew that the king was passing by in the royal carriage with his beautiful daughter. When the carriage rumbled onto the bridge, the cat called out "Help, help, the Marquis of Carabas is drowning!"

The king's servants rushed to the miller's son and helped him out of the water and into some fine new clothes. He was put in the carriage with the king and the princess. The king was delighted to meet the Lord who had been sending him so many gifts and the princess thought him very handsome, too.

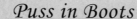
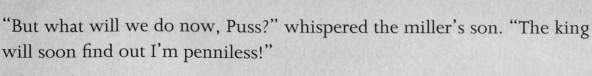
"But what will we do now, Puss?" whispered the miller's son. "The king will soon find out I'm penniless!"

"Leave it to me," purred the cat and ran off up ahead. He saw the people of the land mowing in the fields. "Quick!" the cat cried. "The king is coming. If you don't tell him this land belongs to the Marquis of Carabas, he'll chop your heads off!"

The people were so afraid, they did what they were told. When the king asked whose land it was, they all said, "It belongs to the Marquis of Carabas."

Next, the cat came to a mighty castle. Puss knew that an ogre with magical powers lived there. The cat knocked at the door and the fearsome ogre answered. "What do you want?" the ogre boomed. "I am busy preparing a great feast."

"Is it true, mighty ogre," asked the cat, "That you can change yourself into anything?"

"It is," said the ogre. "Watch." Suddenly, the ogre turned himself into a terrible roaring lion, who chased Puss all around the castle.

Finally the ogre became tired and changed back into his own form.

"That's very good," said the cat, "but I bet you can't turn yourself into something small, like a mouse."
"Of course I can!" bellowed the ogre. He turned himself into a tiny mouse and straight away, Puss jumped on him and ate him up!

Just then, the royal carriage rolled up to the door. "So, is this your castle, Marquis?" asked the king to the miller's son. Before the miller's son could reply, Puss said, "Yes, Your Majesty, it is, please step inside."

The king marvelled at the splendour of the castle and so did the miller's son, who'd had no idea of Puss' plan. While they ate the magnificent feast the ogre had prepared, the princess whispered something to her father.
The king said to the miller's son, "Marquis of Carabas, I would be honoured if you would take my daughter's hand in marriage."

So, the miller's son proposed to the princess and they were married within a week. The miller's son became a prince and the cat was rewarded with as many mice as he could eat – and a new pair of even brighter, shinier boots.

After that, the miller's son, the princess and Puss lived happily ever after.

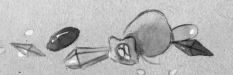

The Sprites and the Dragon

Once upon a time, a grim, old dragon lived in a cave high in the mountains. This dragon was almost as ancient as the mountains themselves. Once his scales had been deep bronze, but now they were greenish and faded. He was lean and scaly and his eyes glowed red like coals on a fire. Every animal for miles around was scared of the dragon.

The dragon had a pile of treasure, that he loved to sit on top of. It filled up his huge, echoing cave and was full of helmets and weapons from defeated knights, shimmering jewels and thousands of gold coins.

One gloomy day, the dragon was counting his jewels when he heard a high, chattering sound. Something small, green and giggling came into his cave. It was a skinny wood-sprite from the forest. "Let's live here now!" piped the sprite and suddenly, a whole crowd of sprites came pouring into the dragon's cave.

Nothing the dragon could do would get rid of the dancing, chattering sprites. And being shadowy little things, they couldn't be swiped with his claws or burned with his fiery breath. Every day, more and more sprites appeared, until the dragon couldn't sleep at all.

"Why are you here?" he asked the sprites. They told him that they had been chased out of their forest home by wolves. "We will live here, now," they squeaked," which made the dragon snort flames in surprise.

The next day, the dragon could take no more. He flew down from the mountains like a storm cloud, all the way to the forest. He searched for the wolves, but he was too big and they were too quick and clever for him. All he could see was their yellow eyes, staring at him from between the trees.

In a clearing, the dragon a woodcutter. The woodcutter was terrified and tried to run, but the dragon landed in front of him. "Tell me, woodcutter," roared the dragon. "Why do the wolves chase things out of this forest?"

"Because they want it all to themselves," replied the woodcutter. "We used to hire men to drive them away, but robbers took all our gold and nobody will help us now."

The dragon snorted and flew away, leaving the poor woodcutter trembling.

The Sprites and the Dragon

On the edge of the forest, the dragon found a family crowded into a tiny cottage. The mother and father shrunk back in fear when the dragon poked his long head through their door, but the children laughed and reached out to touch his snout.

"We have no fence, so the wolves came and stole our sheep," said the father. "They have eaten all the sheep and we are afraid we will be next."

The dragon snorted a second time and flew away, thinking.

On a high hill, the dragon saw a man dressed in battered old armour. This man didn't run away when the dragon landed. "I am a knight," said the man bravely. "If my armour was new, I would try to slay you and the wolves. But all my armour is rusted and useless."

The dragon snorted again and flapped slowly back to the mountains.

"If I get rid of the wolves in your forest, will you leave?" said the dragon to the sprites. The sprites said that they would.

The next day, the dragon flew back down to the forest and dropped something at the woodcutter's feet. It was a huge, red ruby from his pile of treasure. "Sell this to find men to drive the wolves away," said the dragon.

Then the dragon spent an hour slashing at some tall trees with his claws, until he had a huge pile of wood which he bought to the farmer and his family. "Use this wood to build a strong fence to keep the wolves out," said the strong dragon.

Lastly, he flew back to his cave and picked up the toughest, shiniest armor, sword and helmet he could find. He brought it to the knight. "Wear this, but don't fight me," said the dragon. "Use it to drive the wolves away."

"I will if you will help me," said the knight.

So, the knight darted into the deep forest and chased the wolves out and the dragon blew flames at them until the wolves scampered away in fright.

Later, the dragon visited the shepherd and his family. They had built a strong fence in case the wolves returned. "Now we're safe," said the farmer. "But we have no sheep. I don't know how we'll survive."

So, the dragon picked up wild sheep from the mountains in his great claws and dropped them into the fenced field. The shepherd and his wife thanked him, but the dragon was already flying back to his cave.

"The wolves are gone," said the dragon to the sprites in the cave. "Now leave!"

The sprites cartwheeled down the mountain and into the forest and the dragon sat down to guard his treasure in silence.

But something wasn't right. It was too quiet. Try as he might, the dragon couldn't get comfortable. What was the point of all his treasure he thought, if it didn't do anyone any good?

So the dragon flew back to the forest and was glad to see that the woodcutter, the farm family, the sprites and even the knight cheered when they saw him again. "You all need protecting more than my treasure does," rumbled the dragon. "And perhaps I was a little lonely in my old cave."

So, the dragon stayed in the forest. He carried his treasure down from the mountain and buried it deep under an oak tree. But when the people of the forest were in need, they sometimes found a great ruby on their doorstep, or an ancient gold coin lying in their fields as if it had been dropped there by the dragon.

They say that the dragon still guards the forest. So if you ever go into a forest and hear a sound like a fiery snort, or see a glint of bronze, don't worry; it's just the dragon, protecting you from the wolves.

The Boy Who Cried Wolf

Once upon a time, there lived a young shepherd boy. Every day, he took his sheep up the side of a mountain and let them graze. Every night, he took the sheep back down to their pen in the farm. All day long, the shepherd boy watched the sheep. It was very dull. "I wish I had some other people up here with me," he thought. "But nobody wants to walk all the way up the mountain, just to see me."

So, the shepherd boy ran down the mountain to where his older brother was farming the land, with several big farm workers helping him. "Help, a wolf is attacking my sheep!" cried the shepherd boy, jumping around and waving his hands.

At once, his brother and the farm workers rushed all the way up the mountain, puffing and panting. "Where's the wolf?" they cried. "There's no wolf," admitted the shepherd boy. "It was just a joke."

His brother and the farmhands went back down the mountain, in a very bad mood. The shepherd boy just giggled. "That was fun," he thought.

The Boy Who Cried Wolf

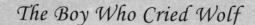

The next day, the shepherd boy decided to try his trick again. This time, he ran all the way down into the small village by the farm.

"Help, a wolf is attacking my sheep!" he cried. "Come, quickly."
All the people in the village followed the shepherd boy up the hill.

"Ha, ha, there's no wolf," said the shepherd boy, when the people from the village reached the sheep. "It was just a trick." The shepherd boy rolled around on the grass, laughing, while the villagers left, angrily.

The next day, the shepherd boy decided to try his trick on an old shepherd who lived on the other side of the mountain. He ran round to the shepherd and cried, "Help, a wolf is attacking my sheep!"

The old shepherd looked hard at him, until the shepherd boy had to look away. "You're lying," said the old shepherd. "Now leave, before I set my sheepdog on you!"

The shepherd boy ran away, annoyed that his trick hadn't worked.

The next day, the shepherd boy saw a big, grey shape slinking behind his sheep. It was a wolf.

Quick as a flash, the shepherd boy ran down the mountain to the farm.

"Wolf! Wolf!" he yelled. "There's a wolf on the mountain."
His brother and his brother's friends laughed at him. "We're not going to fall for that one again," his brother said.

So, the shepherd boy dashed into the village. "Please, help me!" he cried.
"A real wolf is attacking the sheep."
"Go away," said the people of the village. "We don't have time to listen to your lies."

In despair, the shepherd boy ran back up the mountain. He saw that the wolf was sneaking closer and closer to the sheep.

The shepherd boy ran round the mountain to where the old shepherd sat with his sheepdog. "I know you won't believe me!" cried the shepherd boy, "but a real wolf is about to attack my sheep!"

The old shepherd stared hard at the shepherd boy and the shepherd boy thought he was going to send him away again. "Come on, then, boy," said the old shepherd, grimly. "There's not a moment to lose." They ran back round the mountain with the old shepherd's sheepdog.

When the sheepdog saw the wolf, it ran at it, growling. The wolf jumped back in surprise and then ran off, its tail between its legs.

After thanking the old shepherd, the shepherd boy went down into the village. He told everyone what had happened. "I'm sorry I lied to you all," said the shepherd boy, sadly. "I don't blame you for not believing me when I said a wolf was attacking my sheep. I'll never lie again."

Soon after, the old shepherd called the shepherd boy around to his side of the mountain. In the old shepherd's hut, the sheepdog had had six tiny puppies. "Take one," said the old shepherd. "It'll help you guard the sheep."

The shepherd boy chose a black and white puppy. It grew up to be a loyal sheepdog and together, the shepherd boy and his dog guarded the sheep well.

After that, the shepherd boy was never lonely. He didn't tell any more lies and he never cried, 'Wolf,' again.

The Boy Who Cried Wolf

The Clockwork Knight

O nce upon a time, there was a poor toymaker who had one son and no daughters. The toymaker made wonderful toys such as wind-up dolls that walked, wooden dragons that roared and puppets that seemed almost real. But the toymaker sold his toys for so little that he and his son hardly had enough to eat.

One day, the toymaker's son, whose name was Peter, heard about a great treasure inside a huge fortress guarded by a dragon. It was many days' journey away. "I must go and find the treasure," said Peter. "Then we will no longer be poor."

"Before you go," said the toymaker said, "I will make you a companion who will keep you safe from harm." The toymaker toiled in his workshop for many days. With his last pennies, he bought sheets of brass and made them into arms and legs. He took clockwork wheels and made them into a clockwork heart and mind. He took a brass helmet and beat it into the shape of a face. When he was done, he had created a knight made of clockwork, as big as Peter. The knight moved stiffly, but he could walk and talk and even fight with his brass sword.

Peter and the clockwork knight set out on their journey.

At the end of the first day, they camped on stony ground. "Go to sleep," said the clockwork knight, "And I will watch for danger." The clockwork knight did not need to sleep and he guarded Peter all night.

The next morning, Peter wound up the clockwork knight with the big key in his back and they set off again. As they were travelling through a rocky pass, they were attacked by two long-eared, long-nosed trolls.
The clockwork knight drew his gleaming brass sword and struck the trolls down before Peter could even move.

"Thank you for saving me," said Peter. "You are a brave companion."
The clockwork knight bowed stiffly.

Peter and the clockwork knight continued their journey for many days, until they came to a fortress with a wide moat all round it. From a window in the very highest tower, Peter could see the glint of gold.

"The treasure is inside," said Peter. "How can we get across the moat? I can't swim."

"Neither can I," said the clockwork knight. "But maybe I do not need to." Without another word, the clockwork knight walked into the moat. Because he was clockwork, he needed no air to breathe. So, he was able to walk across the bottom of the moat and come out the other side. Then he let down the draw bridge so that Peter could walk across.

Inside the castle, a mighty dragon guarded the gateway that led to the tower and the treasure. It was an ugly dragon with great fangs that curved down past its gigantic jaws.

Peter grabbed his sword. "It's time for me to fight the dragon," he said, nervously. "Wait," said the clockwork knight. The knight whirred all the cogs and gears of his clockwork mind to work out a way to get past the dragon and soon, he had an idea. "Master," he said to Peter, "When you see that the dragon is distracted, run to the gateway."

Before Peter could reply, the clockwork knight ran up to the dragon, brandishing his sword. When the dragon tried to grab the clockwork knight in its claws, the knight did nothing. Instead, he let the dragon bite at his brass body with its long fangs. "Run up the stairs, Master!" called the clockwork knight.

But Peter could see that the dragon was damaging the clockwork knight. With a great yell, Peter ran at the dragon and swiped his sword at the dragon's belly. Howling in pain, the dragon dropped the knight and flew off into the sky, far into the distance.

Peter knelt by the clockwork knight. The knight was dented and scratched and his legs were so bent that he could hardly stand.

"Why did you save me?" asked the clockwork knight. "You could have run through the gateway and got the treasure."

"You saved me from the trolls and you crossed the moat for me," said Peter. "You're a true friend, and friends don't leave each other behind."

 Peter helped the clockwork knight up the stairs to the room at the top of the tallest tower. Treasure was piled in big heaps – emeralds, sapphires, rubies and all kinds of golden chains, crowns and bracelets. In one corner, there was a great fireplace filled with fierce flames.

 "You will have to leave me here," said the clockwork knight sadly, "My legs are too bent to carry me home."

 "Perhaps," said Peter, looking at all the gold, "and perhaps not."
That night, Peter melted all of the gold in the fierce flames. He hammered it into the shape of legs and then took the clockwork knight's old brass legs off and then fixed the golden legs to the knight.

 "Try them," said Peter. The clockwork knight stood up. He moved his new golden toes, then his golden feet, then his golden knees. He found that he could walk, hop and even run! He did a funny clockwork jig for joy.
"My new legs are perfect," said the clockwork knight, "now we can go home."

 Peter and the knight gathered all the treasure that they could carry. They journeyed for many days, all the way back to the toymaker's house and the clockwork knight kept watch over Peter every night, his golden legs gleaming in the moonlight.

 When the toymaker saw them returning with the treasure, he ran out of his shop and hugged them both. "We will never be hungry again," he said.

 As a reward for his hard work, the clockwork knight was polished until he shone and his clockwork heart swelled so much that it almost burst out of his brass chest. And Peter, the toymaker and the clockwork knight lived happily ever after.

Pinocchio

Once upon a time, an old carpenter, called Geppetto, lived all by himself. He was so lonely, he decided to make a wooden puppet to keep him company.

In his workshop, Geppetto carved a little wooden head, a wooden body and wooden arms and legs. Then he dressed the puppet in clothes, like a real boy. "I will call him Pinocchio," said Geppetto. The old carpenter looked at the puppet. "I wish you were real," he said. "I have always wanted a son."

Suddenly, by some strange, unseen magic, the wooden puppet began to move. Geppetto stared in amazement as it jumped up from the work bench and began to run around the workshop, shouting and waving its arms.

Geppetto was overjoyed. He did not understand why his wooden puppet had come to life, but he was very happy. "Pinocchio," said Geppetto, "I am your father and tomorrow you will go to school. Maybe, one day, if you learn enough, you will become a real boy."

That night, when Pinocchio went to bed, he dreamed that a beautiful fairy visited him. "I am the Blue Fairy who looks after all boys – real, or wooden," she said. "I have brought you a friend to help you to be good." The Blue Fairy waved her wand and a tiny cricket appeared.

The cricket was able to speak. "Hello, Pinocchio," it said. "I will be your friend and help you to behave properly, like a real boy. Tomorrow, we shall go to school together."

The next morning, Pinocchio went downstairs with the cricket. Geppetto was very proud that his little wooden son was going to school. "Here are five gold coins to buy school books with," he said. "It's all the money I have in the world, so spend it wisely."

"Yes, Father," said Pinocchio. But the wooden puppet was lying. He did not want to go to school, or spend the money on school books. Suddenly, Pinocchio's wooden nose grew longer. Geppetto looked at it and frowned. "Pinocchio," he said, "why is your nose growing?" But the puppet just grabbed the gold coins, shoved them into his pocket and ran out of the door.

The clever cricket knew that the puppet's nose had changed because he had told a lie. From that moment on, each time Pinocchio lied, his nose grew longer.

Meanwhile, outside the house, Pinocchio heard lovely music. "Let's go to school," said the cricket, but Pinocchio ignored him and followed the music, which led to a travelling puppet theater.

"I am going to stay here and become a performer," said Pinocchio. "My father won't mind." But when he said this, Pinocchio's nose grew, which meant he was lying.

The cricket tried to stop Pinocchio, but the puppet would not listen.
Instead of going to school, he travelled with the theater to a distant land,
near the sea.

Poor Geppetto looked everywhere for his precious, wooden son.
But Pinocchio was nowhere to be found.

After many days, the cricket persuaded Pinocchio to go back home.
They set off and Pinocchio jangled Geppetto's five, gold coins in his pockets,
as he walked.

Nearby, a cunning cat and a sly fox heard the money jangling.
"Where are you going, little wooden boy?" they asked. Pinocchio told them
that he was going home to see his father. "Your father will make you go to
school, when you could be having fun in the Land of Play," said the sly fox.

"However," said the cat. Nobody who has any money can get in.
Money isn't allowed in the Land of Play."

Pinocchio gave the fox and the cat all of his money. He would not listen to the cricket who told him not to. "Tell me the way to the Land of Play," begged Pinocchio, "I want to go there now."

The cat and the fox told Pinocchio where to go. Then they ran off, laughing at how they had tricked the silly puppet out of his money.

"Please, Pinocchio, go home to your father," pleaded the cricket. "I don't want to see my father," snapped the puppet. Suddenly, his nose grew longer. Pinocchio secretly missed Geppetto, but he refused to go home.

The Land of Play was a huge fair. There were sweets and rides and lots of games to play. It was filled with children who didn't want to go to school and Pinocchio spent many weeks there.

Meanwhile, Geppetto was sick with worry. He searched all over the land for Pinocchio, but there was no sign of him anywhere. Finally, Geppetto reached the sea. "Pinocchio must have crossed the water," he thought. Geppetto built a raft to look for his son. However, far out on the ocean, the raft was swallowed by a huge shark and Geppetto found himself in its belly.

In the Land of Play, Pinocchio didn't notice the days passing until his ears began to feel strange. They were long and floppy, like donkey's ears. Then, when he looked behind him, Pinocchio noticed that he had grown a donkey's tail.

"All children who stay here turn into donkeys," said the cricket. "We must escape, before you become one, too, Pinocchio."

However, the gates of the Land of Play were shut. The only way out was by sea, so Pinocchio and the cricket jumped into the water.

Great waves rolled and the wild sea tossed the pair up and down. After many hours, a huge shark swam by and swallowed the exhausted friends.

It was dark inside the shark's belly. Suddenly, Pinocchio heard a voice – it was Geppetto! "I'm sorry that I lied and ran away, Father," sobbed Pinocchio.

Geppetto hugged his wooden son. "I forgive you," he said. They all danced for joy and the movement gave the shark such a belly-ache, it spat them out and they were washed up on the shore.

After that, Pinocchio promised to be good and this time, his nose didn't grow. Instead, the Blue Fairy appeared. "Pinocchio, you have learned to tell the truth," she said. "Now you are a real boy."

Pinocchio felt the donkey ears and tail disappear. Suddenly, his wooden body was soft and warm. He was a real boy! Pinocchio, Geppetto and the cricket returned home and lived in peace and happiness ever after.

The Sword in the Stone

A long time ago, a knight called Sir Ector lived in a great castle Sir Ector had two sons. The older one was named Kay and the younger one was called Arthur. Kay was training to be a knight. Arthur would work as Kay's squire.

While Kay learned all the skills of knighthood, Arthur had to clean Kay's armor, feed Kay's horse and do anything that Kay asked. At dinner, Kay got to sit at the head of the table with Sir Ector, while Arthur was made to sit far away at the other end. Sir Ector was a good man, but he didn't understand that Arthur was leading a miserable life.

One day, while Arthur was trying to polish Kay's suit of armor with an old rag, when he saw an old man who seemed to have appeared from nowhere. The man had a long, white beard, a set of dusty blue robes and a tall blue hat. "How can I help you, old man?" asked Arthur. "I am your new teacher," said the old man, with a mysterious smile. "I am a wizard and my name is Merlin."

From that day on, Merlin taught Arthur something every day. Because Merlin was a wizard, his lessons were never dull.

One day, Merlin turned Arthur into a bird, so he could learn wisdom from the owls deep in the woods. The next day, Arthur became a dog and learned how to command sheep in the fields.

The Sword in the Stone

"Why are you teaching me these things?" asked Arthur. "I am going to be a humble squire when I grow up aren't I? "But Merlin would just smile kindly and change the subject.

A year and a day after Merlin had arrived, Arthur went to his teacher's room and found that Merlin had packed up all his things. "I am leaving," said Merlin. "I have taught you everything you need to know." "Don't go!" said Arthur. "I still have so much to learn."

Merlin shook his head sadly. "You are ready now," he said. "For what?" asked Arthur, but Merlin wouldn't say.

"I will return one day," Merlin said, "but for now, remember my advice when you are in need of a sword, look in a churchyard." Suddenly there was a crack and a flash of light and Merlin was gone.

Now, as it happened, there was no ruler in the kingdom where Arthur lived. The knights were always fighting amongst themselves and the only thing that brought them together was a competition, each year, to try and pull out a mighty sword that had become mysteriously stuck in a huge stone in the churchyard.

Each knight wanted to be the one to win the competition because the words written on the huge rock said, "Whoever pulls the sword out of the stone shall be King."

Every knight tried to pull the sword from the stone, but it was stuck fast.

Soon, the time came for Arthur's brother, Kay to try and pull the sword out of the stone, like every other knight. However, no matter how hard he pulled, the stone would not move.

"May I try?" asked Arthur, but Kay pushed him away. "You're not even a noble knight," said Kay.

The next day, there was an important tournament. Arthur carried Kay's armor on foot, while Kay rode on horseback. On the way, Kay realised that he had forgotten his sword. "Go back and get it for me," he told Arthur. "And be quick, or I will not be able to fight."

Arthur hurried back to their lodgings, but the house was locked. Everyone was at the tournament.

"What shall I do?" thought Arthur. And then he remembered Merlin's advice. "I must try to find Kay a sword," he thought. So he went into the churchyard where the sword sat in the stone. He pulled the sword and it came out of the stone as easily as a knife is pulled out of butter. Arthur rushed to Kay. "Here," he said. "It's not your sword, but will this one do?"

Kay took one look at the sword and gasped. "It's the sword in the stone!" All the other knights gathered round, forgetting about the tournament. "It's a trick!" they cried. "There must be a mistake. This boy isn't even a knight."

So Arthur, Kay and the rest of the knights returned to the churchyard. Arthur put the sword back into the stone and all the other knights tried to pull it out again. No matter how hard they tried, it wouldn't move. But when Arthur grasped the sword, he removed it from the stone as easily as the first time.

Sir Ector stepped forward. "Arthur, I have something to tell you," he said, gravely. "You are not my son. Your father was Uther Pendragon, King. Before he died, he asked me to adopt you, to keep you safe."

"Hail Arthur!" cried Ector, and all the knights got down on one knee and bowed to Arthur. Even Kay bowed down.

"I am sorry I treated you so badly," said Kay. "Now you are King, I expect you will banish me from your kingdom."

Arthur took Kay's hand and raised him up. "No, Kay," he said. "You are still my brother. You must become one of my knights. I will have a large, round table made, so that wherever my knights sit around it, they will all feel equal."

So Arthur became King. He had many legendary adventures with his knights of the round table and sometimes Merlin returned to give him advice, wisdom and just a little magic!

Sinbad and the Giant

Once upon a time, there was a fearless sailor named Sinbad. Sinbad and his brave crew sailed the seven seas, exploring strange, new lands and always looking for rare and exotic goods to trade. Often, their searches led them into dangerous adventures, but none was as deadly as Sinbad's encounter with the one-eyed giant.

Sinbad was sailing back to his home, with a ship laden with treasure, when a mighty storm blew up. Huge waves rose higher than the mast and crashed down on the deck. Thunder rattled above the ship and lightning blasted down to strike the mast. Sinbad and his men were thrown into the sea. When the storm cleared, the sailors found themselves washed up on a deserted island. There was no sign of their ship.

The crew explored the island, but the only animals they could find were a herd of sheep grazing on a grassy hill. As Sinbad climbed the hill, he saw a mighty fortress on the other side. Its great doors were open, so Sinbad and his men stumbled inside. There they found an empty courtyard. It was lined with tall doors, all of which were closed. Sinbad and his men were exhausted. They soon fell asleep in the courtyard.

Sinbad and the Giant

The sailors woke up to a thundering sound so loud, they thought the storm had returned. But it was not the storm. A flock of sheep had run into the courtyard. They were followed by a mighty giant. It was his footsteps that were making so much noise. The giant was as tall as four men standing on each others' shoulders. He was fierce and foul-smelling and he had a single eye in the middle of his forehead.

The men tried to escape, but the giant had closed the great doors behind them. "What's this?" roared the giant. "I can smell human beings!" The giant peered at them with his huge eye. Sinbad noticed that the giant couldn't see very well. However, the giant managed to grab Sinbad. "You're very skinny," said the giant, throwing Sinbad to the ground. He picked up another man and felt him all over. "Another skinny one," he said, grumpily, throwing the sailor down.

The ship's cook was a much fatter man. He tried to run from the giant, but the giant scooped him up easily. "That's more like it," bellowed the giant. "Tomorrow night, I will make a big fire and roast you for my dinner!" The giant opened one of the big doors and went into his castle, leaving Sinbad and his men trapped in the gloomy courtyard.

The poor cook was terrified that he was going to be eaten. "Don't worry," said Sinbad. "When the giant lets his sheep out tomorrow morning, we'll rush out, too." So, the next morning, when the giant opened his gates to let the sheep out, Sinbad and his men tried to leave. But the giant saw them and slammed the heavy gate shut before they could get out.

That night, when the giant came back in, he made a fire and tried to find the cook. But Sinbad was too clever for the giant. He hid the fat cook in a pile of sheepskins that were lying in a corner of the courtyard. Then, he marched up to the giant. "Look what you've done to me," said Sinbad, trying to sound like the cook. "I'm so frightened, I've become nothing more than skin and bone."

The giant picked Sinbad up. "You're not worth eating," he said. He threw Sinbad and his men some mutton, which they ate, hungrily. "I'll fatten you up, then eat you tomorrow night," said the giant, going to bed inside his castle.

"How will we get out?" asked the fat cook, coming out from under the sheepskins. Sinbad looked at the sheepskins. "I think I have a plan," he said.

The next morning, when the giant went to let his sheep out, he found that Sinbad and his crew had built a big, smoky fire. The giant could hardly see anything. "You're not getting out," he yelled. As he let his sheep out, he felt along each one's back, to make sure it wasn't Sinbad, or his men. "That's funny," said the giant. "I have more sheep than I thought."

The giant didn't realise that Sinbad and his crew had put sheepskins over their backs and walked out on all fours, pretending to be sheep.

Sinbad and his men ran to the other side of the island and chopped down some trees to make big rafts. By evening, they were almost ready to sail.

However, when the giant herded his sheep back to his castle that night, he realised that the men were gone. "I've been tricked!" he boomed and Sinbad could hear it from the other side of the island.

Sinbad and the Giant

The giant stomped all over the island, looking all around with his one, giant eye. As Sinbad tied the last of the logs to the raft, he made sure everyone was on it. "Set sail!" he cried and the men raised the sheepskin sails.

Just as they were pushing off the raft, the giant saw them. He waded right into the sea. The sailors paddled as fast as they could, but the wind kept blowing them backwards. The giant was up to his neck in the ocean, but he raised his huge hands and tried to smash the raft.

"Cut down the mast," cried Sinbad. The sailors were amazed, but they did what they were told. The tall mast of the raft toppled over and struck the angry giant on the head. The giant sunk right to the bottom of the ocean and never troubled anybody again.

"Now we are stuck in the sea without a mast," said the fat cook, sadly. "We'll never get home."
"There's something on the horizon," said one of the men. "It's our ship!"

Sure enough, Sinbad's ship had survived the storm. Sinbad and his men sailed back home with all their treasure and a wonderful story of a one-eyed giant to tell.

Sinbad and the Giant

The Terrible Twins

It was a normal day at school. As usual, Mr Bleak, the strictest teacher in the school, was in a stern mood. He had told the class to be quiet, but he could still hear someone talking. "Is that you, Sykes?" he said to a boy at the back of the classroom.

"It wasn't me, Sir," answered the boy. "It was Albert and Arthur." Mr Bleak looked puzzled and then annoyed. "There are no children called Albert and Arthur in this class, you silly boy."

The rest of the class giggled. "Silence!" shouted Mr Bleak, but there was still talking coming from somewhere in the classroom. Mr Bleak gave a cold, hard look at each pupil and demanded to know who the culprits were.

Everyone turned to look at the back of the classroom. Albert and Arthur were sitting next to each other at a spare table. The whole class could see them clearly, all except Mr Bleak. He simply could not see the two ghosts that were haunting his classroom. Albert and Arthur were two naughty ghosts who loved playing tricks on teachers.

Mr Bleak clapped his hands. "Enough of this childish behaviour," he said. "This morning, we are going to do some algebra."

Some of the children groaned. Mr Bleak picked up a pen. "Now," he said, "I am going to write some sums on the white board and then I'm going to ask you to give me the answers." He turned to the white board and wrote lots of different sums.

Each time someone gave the correct answer, Mr Bleak wrote a harder sum. It took longer and longer to get the answers. The children started looking at the clock. They all wished that the lunchtime bell would ring.

Suddenly, Albert and Arthur left their seats and crept up behind the teacher. They rubbed out the answers to the sums and wrote wrong ones instead. The children laughed and pointed at the white board. When Mr Bleak turned round, he went a funny shade of red. "Who did this?" he shouted.

The Terrible Twins

When the class answered that it was Albert and Arthur, Mr Bleak looked like he was about to explode, "Who are these invisible children," he said, with his teeth clenched, "ghosts?" And then Mr Bleak laughed, as if it was the most ridiculous thing he had ever heard.

But, no sooner had the words left his mouth, when the pens on his desk rose in the air, floated over to the white board and rubbed out everything he had written. Mr Bleak stared with his mouth open and then carried on as if nothing had happened. "Maybe it's time I had a holiday," he thought to himself.

The Terrible Twins

The terrible twins played a prank on Mr Bleak everyday. They nudged his arm when he tried to take the register. They wouldn't let him tidy his desk. As fast as he put things away, they got them out again. They even tied Mr Bleaks shoe laces together, which they found very amusing, indeed.

Mr Bleak didn't know what to make of it. He didn't shout at the children any more because he was too busy waiting for something to happen. In any case, he couldn't blame the children because Mr Bleak never actually saw any of them doing anything. He was beginning to wonder if the children were right. What if there were ghosts in his classroom?

Then, one day, Albert and Arthur were feeling extra mischievous. Mr Bleak was busy tidying books in the classroom, when the naughty twins began to move them around. Mr Bleak couldn't believe his eyes. Next, Albert and Arthur began to moan and howl and wail like ghouls. Mr Bleak was white with fright. Everything in the classroom was moving, all by itself. It was true, the classroom really was haunted.

"Aaaargh!" screamed Mr Bleak, running out into the playground and waving his arms, frantically. He left Albert and Arthur rolling around and giggling, so much they thought they would burst. This was the best fun ever.

"Ahem," said a voice behind the ghost boys. A woman stood in the corner of the room. She wore a long, old-fashioned dress. Her hair was tied neatly in a bun and she wore small, round glasses. "Oh, no," said the twins, looking at each other and then back at the woman. "It's Miss Shiverton." She had been their teacher when they were alive and now she had come back to get them.

The woman spoke. "I warned you," she said, "if you continued to be naughty, I would come back to haunt you. You have played one too many tricks on poor Mr Bleak."

Arthur and Albert looked scared. Mr Bleak was an angel compared to Miss Shiverton. The two naughty ghost twins turned to leap through the door. They just wanted to get away.

The Terrible Twins

"Stay exactly where you are!" said Miss Shiverton, in her sternest voice.
She held out a long, spindly cane. The boys froze. "Come with me, you two
are in detention. There will be no more pranks in this classroom."
The twins hung their heads and turned obediently to follow their teacher.
With that, Arthur, Albert and Miss Shiverton disappeared through the
classroom wall.

After that Mr Bleak was always in a good mood and never shouted.
But sometimes, when the home time bell had rung and the school was quiet,
the corridors echoed with mysterious sounds. Mr Bleak would get shivers
down his spine and run to the exit as fast as he could. After all, he never knew
when the terrible twins might return.

The Tinderbox

Once upon a time, a soldier was returning home from war when he met an old witch. "How would you like to have as much money as you want?" asked the witch.

"I would like that very much," said the soldier.

"Then go down the hole in this tree and you'll find a cave with a door at the end. Open it and you will see a dog who guards a chest full of copper coins. Look around and you will see another door. Behind this is a second dog who guards a chest of silver coins. Next, you will see a third door. Go through it and you will find a dog who watches over a chest of gold coins. If you pick these dogs up and put them on my blue apron, they won't harm you and you can take as many coins as you like."

"How much of this money will be mine?" asked the soldier, amazed.

"All of it. I just want a little old tinderbox that my grandmother left down there. It's a small box with a flint inside, for lighting matches and it is guarded by the third dog."

The Tinderbox

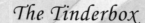

The soldier climbed down into the tree and opened the first door. Just as the witch had said, inside was a dog guarding a chest full of copper coins. "Good doggy," said the soldier, picking up the growling dog and putting it on the blue apron the witch had given him. Filling his pockets with copper coins, the soldier put the dog back and opened the next door.

Inside this room was a second dog who guarded a chest full of silver coins. Plucking up his courage, the soldier grabbed the dog and put it on the blue apron, then he grabbed handfuls of the silver coins.

Opening the door to the last room, the soldier found a third dog, which guarded a chest full of gold coins. It snarled and slobbered, but the soldier picked it up and put it onto the apron. The fearsome dog sat quietly while the soldier filled his remaining pockets with gold. The soldier found the little tinderbox, then made his way back to the hole in the tree.

The Tinderbox

The witch pulled the soldier out of the hole in the tree and asked for the tinderbox. "Why do you want it?" asked the soldier.

"Just give it to me!" screamed the witch and rushed to attack him, her fingernails like daggers. But the soldier was too fast for the witch. Before she could reach him, he drew his sword and chased her away.

Then soldier walked on until he reached a city. With all the money from the hole in the tree, the soldier was rich. He stayed in expensive rooms, bought the finest clothes and food and soon he had made a lot of new friends.

In the middle of the city was a palace. "A princess lives there," said his friends. "It has been foretold that she will marry a common man. But her wicked father, the king, keeps her locked in the palace."

The soldier bought so many expensive things that soon he had hardly any money left. He was forced to leave his rich lodgings and stay in a draughty old attic and all his new friends deserted him.

One cold day, the soldier decided to light a fire. He struck the old tinder box to get a spark and the brown dog appeared!

"What is your bidding, my master?" the dog growled. The soldier was delighted. "Bring me some money," he said and the dog ran off and in a flash returned with a bag of copper coins.

The soldier found that if he struck the tinderbox once, the first dog appeared and if he struck it twice, the second dog appeared. Striking it three times brought the third dog. Soon, the soldier had all the money he could spend again, but all he wanted was to meet the princess. So, that night he commanded the first dog to bring her to him. The dog ran off and reappeared with the princess on his back. She was very beautiful and he kissed the astonished princess' hand before asking the dog to return her.

"I had such a strange dream last night," said the princess at breakfast the next day. When her father the king heard what had happened, he grew suspicious. A serving-maid was sent to watch over her sleep.

The next night, the second dog brought the princess to the soldier. The serving-maid saw the dog take the princess to the soldier's house and she marked the door with a chalk cross.

The next morning, she took the king and queen down to the door. "She went in this house," she said. But all the houses had chalk crosses on! The clever dog had marked every house in the neighbourhood with chalk crosses to confuse the king and queen.

On the third night, the queen tied a bag of flour to the princess' dress. The soldier sent the first dog to bring the princess, but he didn't notice the bag spill flour. The king and queen followed the trail of flour to the soldier's house and had him arrested. The soldier was dragged to prison without his tinderbox.

The next day, the soldier was due to be executed. He called through his prison bars to a passing boy. "Please bring me my tinderbox." The boy brought it and when the soldier was on the scaffold and about to be executed, he asked the king for one last thing. "Could I have one last smoke?"

The king agreed and the soldier brought out his tinder-box and struck it once, twice, three times. The three dogs appeared and chased the wicked king and all his soldiers out of the city. The soldier was free and so was the princess. The soldier married the princess and became king of the city and they lived happily ever after.

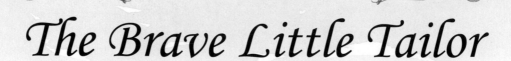

The Brave Little Tailor

Once upon a time, there lived a little tailor who liked to brag about everything he did.

One day, the tailor was about to eat his lunch when he saw that seven flies had settled on it. As quick as a flash, the tailor swatted them all with one blow. "I must be the fastest fly-swatter in the world," said the tailor, proudly. "I want everyone to know how quick and clever I am."

The tailor took a belt and sewed the words "SEVEN IN ONE BLOW" into it. He paraded around his village, wearing the belt, every day. News of the tailor and his unusual belt travelled through the village.

"Maybe it means he knocked down seven men in one blow," said one villager. Before long, everyone for miles around was telling the story of the strong little tailor.

The story even reached the land where giants lived. It fell on the ears of one very mean giant. "So this tailor knocked down seven men with one blow, eh?" the giant rumbled to himself. "I'm going to find him and see how strong he is."

When news of the giant's journey reached the tailor, he was very scared. But soon, he had come up with a clever plan.

The Brave Little Tailor

The giant arrived at the village and the tailor went to meet him. "Great giant," shouted the tailor. "I challenge you to a contest of strength. We'll each carry one end of a heavy tree. Whoever carries it the longest, wins." The giant chuckled. He agreed to the tailors plan, because he knew that he would win.

The giant pulled a huge tree out of the ground. "You take the root end and I'll take the heavier end wth all the branches," shouted the tailor. While the giant was picking up his end of the tree, the tailor climbed into the branches.

The giant picked up the tree and walked across the hills. The tailor kept calling out from the branches, saying things like "Why so slow?" and "Come on, hurry up!" The giant couldn't see the tailor through the branches. Eventually, he became exhausted and fell to the ground.

Meanwhile, the tailor jumped down from the tree. "Great Giant, are you tired?" he asked, leaping around, full of energy. "How can you be so strong?" the giant cried. He was so scared that he ran away and never came near the village again.

The villagers congratulated the brave little tailor on his cunning victory, but the tailor didn't boast about it because he'd learned his lesson. After that, he never boasted again and everyone in the village lived happily ever after.

The Cowardly Dragon

Deep in a forest there lived a cowardly dragon. He breathed fire and had long claws, but the dragon was scared of everything. One day, he heard a loud noise coming from the other side of his hill. It was a boy playing in the wood.

The dragon hid and listened in silence, his heart pounding. "I've never met a boy before," he thought. "What if they're dangerous?"

The dragon was so frightened he started to cry. "Please don't hurt me," he said to the boy, in his deep voice. "You look very dangerous." The boy went up to the dragon and took his claw. "I'm not scary," said the boy. "My name is Tristan. Come with me and visit the town where I live."

Tristan took the dragon back to his town, where everyone welcomed him. The dragon got on well with all of Tristan's friends and family. He felt like he had finally found somewhere where there was nothing to be afraid of.

The only person that wasn't happy to meet the dragon was the town's mean old mayor. "Tristan, why have you brought this monster to our town?" the mayor shouted. "You must be punished! I order you and your family to leave this town and never come back!" All the townspeople gasped, but they were too frightened to say anything. Tristan was so shocked, he started to cry.

When the dragon saw Tristan crying, a strange thing happened. The dragon got very angry. He forgot to feel afraid. He stood up to his full height, towering over the people of the town. He stamped over to the mayor and picked him up in his claws.

"How dare you talk to my friend like that," boomed the dragon. "You should be ashamed of yourself, picking on a nice boy like Tristan. You're nothing but a bully!"

And before the mayor could reply, the dragon threw the mayor up in the air and batted him away with his tail. The mayor flew through the air and landed on Tristan's father's haystack. He was so frightened, he ran out of town and never came back.

With the mayor gone, no one had to live in fear of him anymore. The people of the town gave the dragon a huge shiny gold medal for being so brave. The dragon was so happy, he decided to stay in the town with Tristan and they lived happily ever after.

The Weird Wishes

Karl and Andy stared at the black, wooden box they had just discovered in Andy's back yard. It was about the size of a shoebox and covered in strange carvings. "It looks weird," said Andy, "don't open it."

Karl ignored his friend and tried to pry the lid off. With a loud crack, the lid flipped open. There was a musty waft of air, then a scaly creature flew out and hovered next to them. The creature looked like a lizard, with bright eyes, purple scales, a yellow belly and a long, swishing tail. It had hands like a monkey's paws, and a big, grinning mouth.

"What is it?" gasped Andy.

To their surprise, the creature answered. "I'm a genie," it said.

"You don't look like a genie," said Karl. "Genies come out of lamps. They wear earrings and pointy shoes."

The creature hissed at the boys. "I am not a genie of fairytales," it said. "You have three wishes. What's your first one?"

Before Andy had a chance to speak, Karl blurted out a wish. "I wish we looked like really cool monsters," he said.

"Your wish is my command!" said the genie.

The genie swished its tail and the boys began to shiver and change. Karl had clawed feet, green hair, orange skin and horns coming out of his forehead. Andy was covered in fur and had big ears and fangs. The friends looked at each other in amazement.

When Andy's little sister saw her brother and his friend, she screamed and ran upstairs. "Monsters!" she cried. Andy and Karl went out into the street to see their friends, but their friends yelled in fright.
"Help!" they shrieked. "We're being attacked!"

Everyone on the street stopped and stared at the monster boys. Some people laughed and others screamed. "Get them!" someone cried. "They're monsters!"

The Weird Wishes

"Run!" shouted Andy, and they fled down the street. They heard police sirens and found that they were heading straight towards a parked police car. It screeched to a halt just as they raced down a side street.

The genie was cackling behind the escaping boys. Suddenly, the alleyway turned into a dead end. The policeman chased after them, followed by a big crowd of angry-looking people. "This is horrible," said Karl, "I wish there was a way to fight back!"

"Your wish is my command!" said the genie.

The Weird Wishes

Suddenly, Karl and Andy felt themselves growing. They started to rise above the people, until they were giant-sized. They stepped easily over the brick wall. Karl leaned down towards the crowd and roared, as loud as he could. The people scattered in fear. "That's more like it!" Karl said.
"I'll race you to the top of that tower block over there!" said Andy.

The monster friends easily climbed to the top of the tower block, where they could look over all of the city. They heard a buzzing sound in the distance. It was a swarm of police helicopters, coming to chase them.

Andy tried to swat them as they flew past, but he leaned too far over the edge and lost his balance. "Help!" he cried, as he toppled off the edge of the building.

Karl remembered that he still had a wish. "I wish Andy could fly," he said to the genie. There was a moment of silence and then Andy reappeared, flapping huge bat-wings. The helicopters flew away in fright.

Andy landed and sat next to Karl. "This isn't fun at all," he said. "Everyone hates us and we've used up all of our wishes."

The genie gave a sinister laugh. I like seeing everyone make a mess of their wishes. You've used them up and now you will stay looking like monsters." "Wait," said Andy, "Genie, you granted Karl his three wishes, but what about my three?"

The genie looked annoyed. "Oh, I suppose you can have three, too,"
he grunted.

"Okay," said Andy, "first, I wish we looked like ourselves again."
Karl and Andy shivered, and found that they were back to their normal size
and shape. "Now I wish we were all back in the garden," said Andy.
The genie lashed its tail and a fierce wind blew up. It picked them up and
whirled them back to Andy's back yard.

"And finally," said Andy, "I wish that you, genie, would return to your box
and not come out."

The Weird Wishes

"Nooo!" cried the genie, but it had no choice. With a whoosh, it flitted back into the black box. The lid slammed shut, sealing the genie inside.

"Phew," said Karl, "thanks for using your wishes to save us, Andy."

Andy and Karl buried the box deep in the yard, where nobody would ever find it. Andy switched the portable radio on. "Breaking news," said the announcer, "mystery monsters have run amok in the city!"

"Do you think anyone would believe us if we said those monsters were us?" Karl asked Andy. "We could be famous!"

"You wish!" Andy said, laughing.

The Jester's Quest

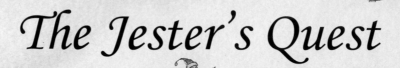

Once upon a time, there was an evil green dragon who lived in a cave in the mountains. This dragon flew around the kingdom, eating sheep, scaring children and sometimes even gobbling up a villager, or two.

The queen summoned all the knights of the castle to appear in her Great Hall. "Is there any one of you who is brave enough to fight the dragon?"

But all the knights stayed silent. They were old and cowardly and they had no wish to fight the dragon.

The queen's jester, sitting at the foot of her throne, laughed at them. "They're no braver than a crowd of kittens, Your Majesty!" This jester was the queen's favourite. He loved to laugh and joke and wave his stick and shake his yellow and red cap covered with bells.

"Then I will choose one of you at random," said the queen. "I make a solemn oath that whomever's name is picked will fight the dragon." All the knight's names were put in a silver box and one was drawn out. The queen announced the name in a loud voice. "The one who is going to fight the dragon is the jester."

The hall fell silent as the jester stepped forward. "But I'm not a knight, Your Majesty," the jester said. "This is some kind of mistake."

"Nevertheless!" said the queen sternly. "You will leave tomorrow to fight the dragon."

On the first night of his journey, the jester stayed at a tavern near a large stone circle. He entertained the people there with acrobatics, but he asked for no payment. Instead, he asked the people of the tavern to cover the stones of the circle with white paint. They were puzzled, but did as he asked.

Next, the jester passed through a rocky ravine filled with enormous boulders. The people came from miles around to hear his jokes but, instead of asking for money, he asked the people to roll a gigantic boulder down the ravine, where it broke in two.

Finally, the jester came to a small village at the bottom of the dragon's mountain. The people here were grim and wary but, nevertheless, they laughed at his stories and his juggling tricks. "Give me no money," said the jester. "Instead, please dig a deep round hole and then dig three triangular holes into the side of it." The villagers were puzzled, but they agreed to do as the jester asked.

The jester said goodbye to them and journeyed all the way up the cold, dark mountain to the dragon's cave. At the entrance to the cave, the jester was almost too scared to go in. "It's no worse than performing in front of the queen," he thought and although this was far from true, it gave him the courage to enter the cave.

Inside, the dragon was crouched on its treasure, growling and spitting and gouging great scratches into the rock with its long claws. "Another knight to challenge me," roared the dragon. "Come here, so I can eat you." The dragon batted at the jester and picked him up in his claws, like a cat picks up a mouse.

"Wait, oh mighty dragon," squeaked the jester. "I'm not a knight. I am here on behalf of the Great Dragon. He wants to challenge you to a fight." "The Great Dragon? I've never heard of him," roared the dragon. But it didn't eat the jester.

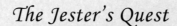

"The Great Dragon wants to find out if you are as strong as he is," the jester said. "That is, if you're brave enough."

The dragon roared like a furnace and huge blasts of flame shot from its nostrils. "Take me to this so-called Great Dragon," said the dragon.

The jester led the dragon down the mountain, to the place where the villagers had dug the big hole. It was so big, the dragon could almost fit in it. "Oh, look," said the jester. "Here is one of the Great Dragon's footprints. He can't be far."

The dragon looked surprised. "I don't care how big he is, I'll beat him."

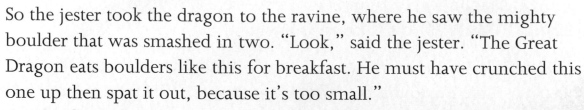

So the jester took the dragon to the ravine, where he saw the mighty boulder that was smashed in two. "Look," said the jester. "The Great Dragon eats boulders like this for breakfast. He must have crunched this one up then spat it out, because it's too small."
For the first time, the dragon seemed nervous. "He certainly sounds very fierce," it growled.

Then the jester and the dragon reached the stone circle that the local people had painted white. "Ah," said the jester, as the dragon wandered around the circle, looking at the huge stones. "This is an old set of the Great Dragon's teeth! He grows a new set every year. This one must be from a few years back, as they're quite small compared to his new set. In fact, I think I see the Great Dragon in the distance."

This was too much for the dragon. It yelped in fright and flew away in fear to a far-off land, where it hoped the Great Dragon would never find it.

The Jester's Quest

The jester chuckled and travelled back to the dragon's empty cave.
He took its treasure and brought it back to the palace. All the knights were
very surprised and the queen was exceedingly grateful.

"There's one thing I don't understand, Your Majesty," said the jester.
"Who put my name in the silver box in the first place?"
"Why, it must have been someone who knew you were the bravest,
cleverest man in the castle," said the queen, smiling secretly to herself.

The jester took his treasure away, but he didn't stop jesting. He became
the only jester in the land who carried a stick made of gold and wore a
silver cap with real gold bells.

The Ice Knight

Once upon a time, there were two brothers called Giles and Roderick. They loved to play with wooden swords and dreamed of growing up to be noble knights. Giles was steady and reliable, but Roderick was sharp-eyed and adventurous.

When it was time for them to leave home, the brothers journeyed in different directions. "We will meet again when we have made our fortunes," they said, shaking hands.

Giles followed the road into a valley. He hadn't been travelling long before he saw a group of robbers. They were attacking a man on horseback. Drawing his sword, Giles ran at the robbers and drove them all away.

The man on the horse was a noble prince. "You're a brave man, you can be my squire," he said to Giles.

Life was hard for Giles. He had to run errands for all the brave knights in the prince's service. But he learned how to fence and how to joust. It took a long time, but eventually he could fight better than any knight.

 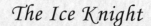 

Meanwhile, Roderick followed a different path. He had heard a legend of a great northern enchanter who was more powerful than any in the land. So Roderick travelled far to the north, to the lands of endless snow, until he found the enchanter's castle which was made of ice. Roderick went inside and found the enchanter on an ice throne, surrounded by blue-eyed snow leopards.

"I will work hard if you will let me serve you," Roderick said.
"You can become a knight straight away," said the enchanter. "Only fools work hard." The enchanter cast a spell, and Roderick found himself in a chilly suit of armor that reflected the pale sun like glass.

The enchanter placed an amulet in the armor's chestplate. "This will give you great powers over snow and ice," he said.

Lastly, the enchanter pulled a great shard of ice from the palace and cast a spell over it. It became a great ice-sword which he gave to Roderick. "Now you are my Ice Knight," said the enchanter. "You must guard my castle from all intruders."

Roderick went to shake the enchanter's hand, but the enchanter moved away. "A human touch means death to me," he said.

Soon, Roderick found that he no longer felt the cold. In fact, the longer Roderick guarded the ice palace, the less he could feel in his heart.

One day, Giles prince told his knights about the enchanter. "This evil man wants to cover all the land in ice. He must be stopped. Who will challenge him for me?" Giles volunteered to go to the north and fight.

When Giles finished the weary journey to the far north, he found the ice castle. Roderick was outside guarding it. He stood as still as an icicle.

When Giles saw his brother, he was overjoyed. But Roderick had forgotten how to feel. "You shall not enter my master's castle," said Roderick. He swung his ice sword at his brother. Giles raised his sword to block it and they began to fight.

Roderick summoned shards of ice and a frozen wind to drive Giles back. But Giles swung his sword and knocked the amulet from the Ice Knight's chest. Now Roderick could not summon snow and ice against his brother. He was forced to use his sword to fight.

Because the ice knight had not worked as hard as his brother, he tired more easily. Soon, Roderick stumbled and fell into the snow. Instead of striking him down, Giles helped his brother to his feet.

The Ice Knight was amazed. "You could have defeated me. Why did you help me?" he asked.

"Because you are still my brother and I love you," said Giles.

Roderick felt his heart melting and all the warmth returning to his body. "I have been bewitched all this time. Let's defeat the enchanter together!" he cried.

They entered the palace to find their way blocked by the snow leopards. "We have been enslaved by the enchanter," said the leader of the snow leopards. "We will fight with you for our freedom."